I0622308

SOULFUL POEMS

AN ANTHOLOGY OF POETRY
ACTIVATING YOUR INNER MENTAL WEALTH

POETS

SPONSORED BY MARK STEPHEN POOLER

KATIE CAREY – DAVID KNIGHT– KATISCHE HABERFIELD –
LALITHA DONATELLA RIBACK

DR. ALEXANDRA MCDERMOTT –AMMA VENTELÄ

ANGELA EVANS – B LOVE SELF – CATHY SHUTER – CAROL
WHITELEY– CINDY LU PORTER – DEBRA PARRY – DENISE
BORLAND – KARLA KOPP – KATIE GAUTHIER – JASNA
STIPANOVIĆ ĐURĐEVIĆ – JULIE CROWDER – MERRYL
SEIBERT – OLIVIA DE SOUSA ROSEY MCBRIDE – DR.
SOLVEIG BERG – SOULI YATES – REV STACEY PIEDRAHITA
STEPH DARMANIN – VICTORIA DUARTE

CREATED BY SOULFUL VALLEY PUBLISHING

Copyright © 2025 by Soulful Valley Publishing and Katie Carey Media Ltd and the Poets within this collaboration.

All rights reserved. Apart from any fair dealing for the purposes of research, private study, criticism, or review, as permitted under the Copyright, Designs and Patents Act of 1988, this publication may only be reproduced, stored, or transmitted in any form or by any means with the prior permission in writing of the copyright owner, or in this case, of the reprographic reproduction in accordance with the terms of licensees issued by the Copyright Licensing Agency. Enquiries concerning reproduction outside those terms should be sent to the publisher.

Other Books by Katie Carey

Available on Amazon now:

Soulful Poems: Heal the Heart and Soul

Entangled No More

Evolving on Purpose: Mindful Ancestors Paving the Way ...

Evolving on Purpose: Co-creating with the Divine

Becoming the Manifesting Diva: Creating Ripples While You Flow

Soulful Poems: A Global Collaboration of Poetry ....

Soulful Poems: Poetry to Activate Your Soul Mission

Soul Warrior: Accessing Realms Beyond the Veil

Intuitive: Knowing Her Truth

I'm So Glad You Left Me: 88 Stories of Courage, Self-Love ...

Let's Celebrate Our Days in Hundreds of Ways!

Visit

https://www.soulfulvalley.com

Disclaimer

The publisher and author provides this book on an "as is" basis and makes no representations or warranties of any kind with respect to the book or its contents. The publisher and the author disclaim all such representations and warranties of healthcare for a particular purpose. In addition, the publisher and the author assume no responsibility for errors, inaccuracies, omissions, or any other inconsistencies herein.

The content of this book is for informational purposes only and is not intended to diagnose, treat, cure, or prevent any condition or disease. You understand that this book is not intended as a substitute for consultation with a licensed practitioner. Please consult with your own physician or healthcare specialist regarding the suggestions and recommendations made in this book. The use of this book implies your acceptance of this disclaimer.

The publisher and the poets make no guarantees concerning the level of success you may experience by following the advice and strategies contained in this book, and you accept the risk that results will differ for each individual. The testimonials and examples provided in this book show exceptional results, which may not apply to the average reader and are not intended to represent or guarantee that you will achieve the same or similar results.

This is a work of creative nonfiction poetry.

Table of Contents

INTRODUCTION

Poetry has always been more than words upon a page. It is the breath between the lines, the heartbeat of truth, and the mirror that reflects our deepest knowing. *Soulful Poems: An Anthology of Poetry Activating Your Inner Mental Wealth* is born from this truth, a gathering of voices, verses, and visions that invite you inward, toward the richest treasure you will ever discover: your own inner wealth.

In a world that often equates wealth with material gain, this anthology whispers a different kind of prosperity. Here, mental wealth is honoured as resilience, clarity, creativity, peace, and connection with something far greater than ourselves. Each poem is a key, a spark, an activation, guiding you to remember that abundance is not only measured in numbers, but in the depth of your awareness, the light of your healing, and the strength of your soul.

These pages hold the wisdom of many poets, souls who have walked through shadow and light, who have transmuted pain into beauty, and who courageously offer their words so that you, too, may remember your infinite worth. Together, we weave a tapestry of hope, inspiration, and inner empowerment, proof that poetry can both soothe and awaken, both comfort and catalyse.

May this collection be your companion in quiet moments, your reminder under challenging seasons, and your spark in times of expansion. Read slowly. Pause often. Let each line touch not just your mind, but your Spirit.

Because your true wealth, the wealth that can never be taken, measured, or diminished, already lives within you. These poems are here to help you see it, feel it, and live it fully.

Katie Carey
Soulful Valley Publishing

MARK STEPHEN POOLER

A Message from Our Book Sponsor

It's always important to listen to your soul, and I am a passionate advocate for authentic collaboration. It's truly my honour to be involved with such incredible, purposeful entrepreneurs through this meaningful project. Poetry comes from the deepest recesses of our souls—it's where truth lives and authenticity flourishes. My passion lies in working alongside soulful entrepreneurs who understand that business success must be rooted in purpose and genuine connection. This book embodies everything I believe in: the power of vulnerability, the strength found in shared stories, and the magic that happens when we dare to express our authentic selves. Always listen to your heart and soul— let that inner wisdom guide your every decision and creative expression.

About Our Book Sponsor

Mark Stephen Pooler

The Global Profile Builder & Architect of Global Influence

As the visionary driving force behind MSP News Global, Mark Stephen Pooler masterfully shapes media narratives while forging powerful connections with global business titans and thought leaders. Before establishing MSP News Global in 2020, Mark carved a distinguished international path as a bestselling author, sought-after keynote speaker, engaging radio and TV host, and astute PR & Media Specialist.

He is the strategic Founder of TMSP Agency, a premium media and PR consultancy where he empowers high-profile entrepreneurs, executives, and visionaries to amplify their authentic stories and achieve worldwide recognition through innovative PR strategies and cutting-edge digital media solutions. Mark's expertise lies in transforming personal brands into global movements, helping clients build influential platforms that create lasting impact across industries.

Beyond his world of global influence and media mastery, Mark treasures quiet moments spent with Lilly, his beloved canine companion and creative muse.

Discover how to build your global profile:

www.contactmark.me

KATIE CAREY

Mental Wealth

We've all heard many stories now,

Of people's struggles with Mental Health,

But what if we flip the focus today,

On creating Mental Wealth?

Stop focusing on negative symptoms,

That keeps our heads in a spin.

Begin to focus more,

On feeling wealthy and worthy within.

Those symptoms we're resisting,

They are trying to keep us safe in our space.

What if we chose to welcome them,

Thank them and give them grace?

We could learn to breathe more deeply,

Trust our bodies know just what to do.

Stop pushing down our darkest emotions,

Instead, allow them to flow through.

This focus on our Mental Wealth,

Holds a frequency within,

That will immediately lift us up

Creating a reality where we can all win.

If we all become so self-aware,

That we know how and why we feel,

That whatever is coming up for us,

We pay attention to what is real.

We notice what these feelings are,

We remember when we've felt them before,

This pattern thinks it is serving us,

When we see it, we can heal and restore

Ourselves back to who we really are,

Open to loving our lives more instead

of always focusing on being scared.

Waking up resentful, hurt, filled with dread.

We have choices available every day,

To care about our Mental Wealth.

Who could we be if we focus on this?

It's time we learned to really love ourselves!

You Are the Purpose!

You've spent years, decades even,

Shifting and changing,

Moving and Grooving

In search of YOUR PURPOSE

Running around chasing the next shiny thing

But maybe if you STOP and PAUSE

Take the time NOW

To slow down, breathe more deeply

Connect with more presence.

In your current reality

With the people, places and things that matter to you the

most

Instead of trying to escape from it

You may remember

Who you are, what you are

and that really

YOU are the PURPOSE

Flowing, Living, Breathing, Connecting

With every pause and every INSPIRED action

Stardust in the Ripples

"For every soul we've loved and lost

may their ripple live on in us."

This beautiful soul has gone too soon

And as we sit in silence, we gaze at the Moon

Why does it ache when Love runs so deep?

Why do the stars sometimes lull us to sleep?

Yet under the sorrow, Love softly glows

It rises around us, above us, it knows.

This soul was rare, radiant, and kind

A spark in the dark, a brilliant mind

We'll never forget the minutes or years

The laughter, the mischief, the joy, and the tears.

We felt their excitement, their zest for the ride

How they rose through the shadows with Love as their

guide.

Some souls create ripples too vast to explain

Magnetic with passion, yet touched by life's pain

Some are called early, too soon for our hearts

As babies, as children, before their new starts.

In our humanness, we ask the same why

But stars don't explain when they fall from the sky.

We're all on a journey, a soul-timed plan

No one can know where it ends or began

So live with intention, feel all you feel

Let the waves crash; healing is real.

And when you've wept, pause and recall

They're never truly gone at all.

They were so special,

so bright

so divine

That Spirit said softly,

"Your mission's done. It's time."

So now we grieve

We ache, we sing

Because the echo of Love

It is a sacred thing.

Speak their name forever, out loud.

Let their ripple remind you.

Love like that never truly leaves.

A Little Girl Who Loved Her Dad

I'm ready to share a story

about a little girl who loved her Dad

About how his life tortured him

Leaving him angry and often mad.

She didn't understand then,

What he was going through

But all the while she loved him

Not knowing what to do.

Then one day, that little girl grew up
She had children of her own
She looked back and wondered why he tortured
All of them at home?

He died too young to talk about
What drove him so insane
Why did he choose alcohol
To numb all of his pain.

She didn't speak to him
For most of his last year
Then the day after Father's Day
She'd face her darkest fear.

He died at only 48
She didn't have the time
To tell him she'd forgiven him
For his lifetime full of crime.

Now she is a grandma herself

And wants you all to know.

Life's far too short for bitterness.

And resentment, it's bad for your health.

So open up your heart today.

Let those emotions stream through you.

And today's the day to forgive yourself

For not knowing what to do.

Your Health is Your Wealth

A virus has come and knocked on my door

My voice has now gone

And my nose is so sore

It's time to listen to my body now

It's been creeping up for days

And I managed somehow.

I have enough content for the rest of this year

There's no need to keep pushing

There's nothing to fear

It's time to be selfish

To take care of me

My body needs to be loved tenderly

A book launch is coming

I'll need energy for that

More poetry is flowing

to be heard - that's a fact

When I slow down, NOW

 I'm allowing myself

To put myself first,

care about my own health

Decades of trauma and mind programming

Makes us feel bad when we're cancelling

But this is the lesson,

Pay attention to yourself

It's not about what others think

When it comes to our health.

If we don't make ourselves the priority

No one is coming to save you or me

We must pay attention enough to care

Love ourselves more, be energetically aware.

The game will change when we observe the self

Listen to her now – as your health is your wealth!

About the Poet

Katie Carey is a publisher, poet, podcast host, and intuitive mentor. As the founder of Soulful Valley Publishing, she has helped over 100 authors become bestsellers. She is featured in the international award-winning movie *Zero Limits*. Through her books, poetry, and globally ranked Soulful Valley Podcast, Katie inspires healing and creative expression worldwide.

Connect with Katie below:

https://pensight.com/x/soulfulvalley

DAVID KNIGHT

The Pool Of Love

Now contemplate and reflect ... as you gaze into the pool,

For the vision and the quest belong not to any fool.

Casting stones across the water, with a weight of
expectation,

May cause ripples of discontent to reach the shores of
many nations.

The crystal-clear divide forms the tears that fill your eyes,

Fear of pain in heart or body ... which most do you
despise?

And as teardrops salt your lips, loving memories you may
miss,

Leaving traces in your mind, though true insight is not
blind.

The reality of your being, deep inside my Love's embrace,

Is eternal for you all, every being and human race.

All life is loved and sacred, every form and not just parts,

Universal and beyond, born way before the stars.

Walk a path of truth, not sin ... guiding light reigns deep
within,

Don't fear to tread the new, as I'll guide you on and
through.

The abyss of doubt and change ... are false emotions in
the way,

For each step that you now take, know you're safe each
night and day.

Should you ask if the pool is shallow ... well, only you can
trust your faith,

Brings peace and joy and comfort, or do you feel your
souls at stake?

It's up to you to test the water, question if I'm real or

fake...

Judge only through your heart, is all I ask you make.

Know choice is my creation, and I've instilled it in you

too,

For the pool will soothe and tend you, not make you cold

or blue.

Come bathe in your Divinity, and rise like brilliant

sparks,

This legacy of your lifetime ... please leave smiles, not

broken hearts.

An Eternal Longing

You are my child of light,

A love supreme ... a sheer delight.

More than a body and eclipsing the mind,

You're unique and beautiful ... forever mine.

Though not a possession ... or something that's
forgotten,
Beyond simple waves, of one's imagination.
With a heart that's full of Love... and the truth that it
now brings,
Upon planes and all dimensions ... beautiful echoes ring
and sing.

Know everyone's a lifeform, and a special part of 'me',
Each is like a leaf ... upon the branches of a tree.
So, open now your eyes, of the heart and mind and soul,
To understand the purpose ... the real road and your true
goal.

One's Divinity was always there, not born from any start,
Etched stronger than a memory ... like blood flowing
through your heart.
Understand I am the energy, and the cause of all creation,
And exist and ebb and flow, like the seas that touch the
nations.

So, please now understand, the who and what you are,

No need to search afar ... nor beyond the stars.

For inside you here I am, just listen and don't look,

Within the silence you will find me ... an open not closed

book.

Each day is an opportunity, a new page of your diary,

Learn to live life to the full ... and be way more ...

carefree.

Non-attachment to the world, and everything that's fake,

Having faith in your true self ... and in me is no mistake.

So, drift if you now must, inside the dreams of thought

and sleep,

Knowing you lay within my arms ... and are safe inside

my keep.

Forever closer than close ... and always nearer than near,

The steps that you now take are no longer tread in fear.

I am by your side ... and within and also out,

Live in peace, keep calm, and never be in doubt.

For your hand is held in mine, as I sing you lullabies,

My dear child, you are so sweet ... and perfectly divine.

Remember, no separation or division, for how can there

be,

When entwined and eternal, you remain at one with me.

Now release all of the pain, and make a brand new start,

As the puzzle is complete ... not doubting we're apart.

Jewels

The abyss and blackness of the cosmos ... deep space,

Are more than a memory, to remind the human race.

For 'within' you lies the answer to real joy and peace and

bliss,

A hunger for truth and freedom ... the reality you can't

miss.

Because inside the peace and stillness, resides no sadness
or wide frowns,

The realisation that you adorn, my heart and soul and
crown.

You are each a priceless jewel, so precious to behold,

Born from Love and not below ... nor above, you are
now told.

Every soul is safely hung, by threads of golden light,

Suspended and now glorified, each shining oh so bright.

One may think they truly see, by day or dark of night,

But the truth can't be seen, only by your sight.

Vision of heart and soul and mind must in unison be,

You'll know that we are 'one'... when you're combining
all three.

A needle in a haystack is so hard to find and true,

But the 'I' that's all of me ... are just reflections of the real
you.

Begin to recognise the difference ... of the truth and
what's fool's gold',
As I lift and always cradle you, as the heavens have
foretold.
You do not have to find or decipher sacred text,
As Love is plain and simple ... and simply is the best.

Broken hearts know I will heal, and I promise not to
leave,
When you trust in 'self' and me ... and decide to now
believe.
In the brilliance of your radiance, allowing creativity to
flow,
Sharing the wonder that's inside you, so that others
surely grow.

In turn, they'll soon discover their own wisdom to also
know,
Continuing this theme ... until everybody glows.
Pure vibrations, Love and energy, will then encompass all

the Earth,

Forget both creed and colour ... rich and poor and meek

and mirth.

Understand the beauty of your truth, is so wonderful to

share,

But only if you mean it, and if you truly care.

For like footprints in fine sand, which can fade and

disappear,

Or can leave eternal traces ... away from pain and the false

fear.

And while the death of previous bodies has cast shadows

and past lies,

Only the shell and beautiful casing, does cease and fade

and die.

Know one's soul cannot be buried, nor burnt or raised

away,

Eternally in my arms ... and in my heart you'll always

stay.

No Escape?

Are you hiding?

Are you afraid?

Are you lost?

Are you sad?

Who or what are you running from?

And in the search you sometimes ask ... "Oh, where do I belong?"

Please don't attempt to disappear ... and hide like a chameleon,

Just shine through darkened clouds ... to glow just like the Sun (Son).

In truth, there's no escape, no veil or false dark curtain,

For I am the eternal witness, of this you can be certain.

You may think you walk alone, upon the trials of path or road,

But I am always, always with you, no need to shout or
use a phone.

The proof is all around you, hear the whispers through
the trees,
My compassion and my mercy ... bestowed without one's
bended knee.
I'll hold your hand forever, even through so-called
'mistakes',
Allow the trust and faith inside you ... to carry every step
you make.

And when you listen to hear my voice, in birdsong, wind
and rain,
I'll bathe you with my grace, through every struggle and
your pain.
My Love is unconditional, and eternal this is true,
Inside you I reside, and I speak to you this truth.

So, I urge you not to hide and never live in fear,

Stop the sadness and be glad ... and wipe away all of those

tears.

Because you'll find me in a smile, or by a stranger's

helping hand,

It's time to live your life, and time to make a stand.

Flow

Rain, lake, river to the sea,

I am Source, one God ... if you can believe.

For truth lies deep within ... clouded not by atmosphere,

But by confusion and illusion, the acceptance of doubt

and fear.

Earth, cosmos, the Universe and time,

Planes and dimensions ... what now shall you find?

Is it hatred and anger, more death and more crime...

Or, my Love and my light, all creation that is mine?

So, will you force and keep on pushing ... to make it up
the stream,
Or, effortlessly glide and then let go ... you know of what
I mean.
For flow is simply natural, and the pace has not been set,
Live in peace and truth and gratitude ... as we've already
met.

Connected are we all, but are you waiting for my call ...
By denying the true you, you might feel down or even
fall.
For bliss it lies eternal, not beyond the deepest space,
It's inside your heart that I reside ... our special,
wonderous place.

With the tears you sometimes cry, and fall upon your
face,
Leave traces of such joy, they illuminate ... and aren't
fake.

They radiate and they glisten, eclipsing diamonds and
many stars,
Erasing regrets of hurt and past ... future's door is seen
ajar.

It leads and it will guide, to the realisation we are 'one',
For a wave merges with my ocean, when all is said and
done.
You're already totality ... so step forward from the shore,
With the ebb and flow of tide, I'll sustain you
forevermore.

About the Poet

David Knight is a multiple Amazon International Bestselling Author who has helped to conduct spiritual development and healing circles for over 25 years. He has also been a guest speaker—sharing his enlightened experiences to promote oneness; and self-realisation—at various Mind, Body, and Spirit engagements across the UK.

Through inner-dictation, dream interpretation, meditation, mindfulness, pre-cognition, and healing, the books he co-writes with Spirit provide the foundation to discover your path of truth. With a renewed sense of purpose, the Spiritual Guidance and Education directs the seeker to become realised, whereby you perceive what is already there ... the truth within the permanence of life-energy and Love. David is tee-total and a vegetarian, who loves the sunshine, nature, animals, and his wife!

Connect with David below:

https://www.ascensionforyou.com/

KATISCHE HABERFIELD

An Ode to Lorrimor

I'm sorry I could not see you

When I was a little boy.

My mind was elsewhere

As all I wanted was a toy.

The cave was dark and eerie

The fire was all I saw.

But could that have been your shadow

Dancing on the wall?

My brother told me you were a Dragon

But I was unsure.

For no one told me Dragons were real

And not just something your mother drew on the cave

wall.

But once I'd done my right of passage

My wisdom opened up.

Then clear as day I could see you.

Even though it gave me a fright.

I'd best not dwell on what happened next

But I was all alone.

But every night I returned to you

And you became my home.

So thank you for guiding me

Through all of life's ups and downs.

I know some of the things we did

Would surely make my mum frown.

But a boy's got to live and feed himself

And I was only ten.

So I try to think of what to do

And then I saw the fairy wren.

She told me to look up in the sky

To the lights that twinkle bright.

My mother father and brother were there

Waving in the night.

An Angel did as well appear

And told me it was fine.

Because the most important thing to do

Was build myself a den.

And that's how we survived the fire

That raged through the town that night.

And sometimes I felt so sad

To be all alone in the world.

But then you, my dragon would explain to me

That everything would be alright in the end.

So thanks again for helping me

I needed it for sure.

I'm glad you are around for me forevermore.

But now I'm in a different body, and I've never been so
sure
That all the fantasy creatures exist
That's for sure.

So if you feel alone at night
Or if darkness is at your door.
Just remember to call out for help
They'll respond, that's for sure.

At first they might be hard to hear
Or you might doubt yourself.
But soon you will believe in them
And then you will understand
That every fairy tale comes true
If you just read to the end.

So make a wish upon a star
And give yourself some hope.

What is meant for you will come

When the time is right.

Sitting silently

Sitting silently

The trees bend in the wind.

Watching peacefully

I allow my emotions to bend

And move within me.

The movement stills my mind

And allows me to feel the wind

Caressing my cheek.

The bamboo creaks and groans

But I am at peace when alone.

The Wisdom of Fear

Fear eats you from the inside

It twists and knots your stomach

And makes you second-guess yourself.

You lash out

But it laughs back.

You try to contain it

But it grows with every thought.

Pretending it's not there doesn't help

It will creep up and engulf you.

The answer lies in your heart.

Invite fear in for a cup of tea

Infuse it with Love

And treat it like a child who had just sneezed.

Bless your soul my darling.

Are you ok?

Tell me your troubles and worries

And I promise you I'll listen

Even if you have tried to tell me before.

Let me look deep within you.

For I see a light.

Look how beautiful you are.

I'm so sorry you have had to shoulder all that weight for

me.

I love you

Please forgive me

I'm sorry.

Will you take my hand?

Let's try to navigate this again.

What is it that you desire my Love?

It is recognition

It is hunger

It is lust

It is Love

It is union

It is a demand of perfection

Nothing short of perfection.

Then my Love you shall not have it.

For Love is not perfect.

Did you really want the cookie-cutter version of Love?

The Love that came easily and lasted until you died?

You think you did.

But there is nothing to fight for in that kind of Love

No growth, no unmet desires, no exploration, no treasures to find.

You came for the lumpy, the bumpy, the textured

The secret explosion in the middle of the chocolate

The unexpected caramel centre

The piece of cookie dough in the tub of vanilla.

You came for a love that defied the expectations of others.

You came for a love that would baffle others.

But that would light up your soul.

Don't settle or be impatient.

Follow the clues.

Wait.

Scream

Paint, express yourself.

But don't deny yourself the experience because you are impatient.

What if?

What if

The monster under your bed

Was really scared of the tiger

In the bathtub?

What if?

There was a legion of toy soldiers

Ready to battle

If you only called the command?

And what if instead of guns

They had wings?

Some of them looked like Angels

And some looked like bears

Some shimmered like fairies.

What if The only difference between

The monster and the fairy

Was the colour of the light?

Could you open your heart and say

I see you're made of light?

Would you listen to all their worries

And wipe away their tears?

Would you tell them that you loved them

Despite your inner fears?

What if?

Your nightmares

Contained an inner truth

And the child inside you

Just needed the truth.

That some days will be scary

And others will shine bright.

Some come with battles and monsters

And give you a big fright.

But on the days the sun does shine

And sparkles in the sky

There's always a rainbow to be found

In the corner of your eye.

Now some will tell you

That if you focus on your fears they will come true

But what if you liberate them?

And finally see the truth.

The monsters are there to protect you

And help you see the dark

Because the stars need angels

Who can operate in dark

So they can twinkle in your heart.

So when you're feeling all alone

And need someone to hug

Just remember to tell the monster

Come here, you big old thug.

There's something we need to talk about

But I need your point of view

Let's take a balanced approach

And look at what I could do.

I don't want to pretend I'm not worried

But I can feel the fear coming out.

I want to turn it into excitement

So I can work it out.

The thing is I'm not certain

But can you hear me out?

For once I hear your story.

I'm sure to shout and pout.

Because there's an angel

Just standing over there

Who has the opposite opinion

This really isn't fair!

So just let me think it over

And see what I can do.

And so the moral of this story

Is that no matter what you do

There are always monsters and fairies and angels

Waiting to help you think it through.

About the Poet

Katische Haberfield is exploring poetry as a form of direct transmission of her soul's consciousness. Collectively, these moments of inspiration heal her own perception of her soul's journey and she gains inner wisdom from the aha moments that result at the completion of each poem.

She hopes that when reading the poems, you gain insight into your own life, and are inspired to write your own.

Professionally, she is a Spiritual Consultant and Coach, Certified Clinical Hypnotherapist, CHt IPHM, Past Life Regression Therapist, Soul Obstruction Releasement Therapist, Medium, and Channel of the Divine Feminine and Masculine Energies and the Archangels.

Her clients free themselves from the constraints that are holding them back from being the truest expression of who they are, in this lifetime. As well as uncovering invisible obstructions at a soul level.

Tune into her globally ranked spirituality podcast "The Infinite Life" on all podcast players.

Connect with Katische below:

https://katische.com/

LALITHA DONATELLA RIBACK

Thiruchitrambalam

Divine Temple of Consciousness

The ancient bird of war flew proud and high,

On tears of Kurukshetra in silently dreadful sky.

Radiations and corpses bled empty on ground,

Lights went out where vultures' foods were found.

Earth's deep agony and life held still,

Kali Yuga's dark dawn, battles' chill.

Gods withdrew, dust dumped on air,

Broken loves and hopes laid bare.

Lightning slivers cut night's veil,

Tears dry beneath a new Sun's hail.

Stone-cold sorrows lift and clear,

Our galaxy renewed dispels the fear.

My heart I give to sacred bells,

Victories tied with heavenly spells.

All tremors lost, free I dance,

The Moon joins in cosmic embrace.

Angels glide in royal choirs,

Devas with kin, celestial fires.

Heavens rain flowers and shining dew,

Clouds bring forth men born anew.

Glory won, our spirits soar,

Friends shower petals, Love's pure core.

Truth replies to everyone's prayer,

Miracles bloom joyfully everywhere.

Come, walk the quiet path where silence speaks,

Where every heart can find its sacred spark.

Light blooms softly in the soul's embrace,

And peace flows gently through the ending dark.

Step close, where stillness holds a tender flame,

A truth beyond the noise of worldly streams.

There, Love awaits without demand or cost,

Awake within your deep, bright dreams.

When Shiva stills His fearsome, cosmic dance,

The body-temple wakes in radiant trance.

Pure soul aglow, untouched by ugly sin,

Bright gaze reveals the true inner glance.

Simple and splendid is the path,

Follow it in your prana and pure breath.

The lovely Goddess smiles, applauds

To the Friends' delightfully sweet chants.

The Goddess Has Awakened

She Is Golden

The Earth Mother in compassion trembled,

Her baby daughters lost and murdered.

And their mothers chained on slimy rocks,

Their lovely, young heads severed.

Oh Goddess, your rivers of tears abound,

Break through stone walls of olden lies.

Demons die at your hand, free the Universe,

And girls and boys through holes in the ground.

Light seeps through the soil's cracks.

Thunder above and earth breakage,

Chariots in the air, the darkness ravage.

The Mother Divine in her arms wraps.

A crown of flowers on children's heads

The Goddess places with loving touch.

Garlands of foliage on deathbeds.

Free, pink and red colors the women blush.

A crown of gold on the woman, now queen.

The Goddess joins the coronation scene.

A splash of milk drips, the shower of pearls flows.

Petals stick wet on the queen's brows.

Rubies on crown, diamonds on silver,

Silks on the shoulders, scepter in hand,

Hair down the back, eyes of lotus,

Her victory has come, the light shows us.

Her smile outshines the dawn's pure rays,

Garlands of stars entwined in flowing hair.

Golden laughter rings through blossoming days,

The world uplifted in her brilliant Love.

"She is a Witch"

And Millions Died

"She is a witch," all said, laughing at her tears.

"She is a witch," they lamented, cutting her hair.

"What is a witch?" quivered a child taken away.

"She has sinned," screamed the crowd, raising a stone.

She is a witch, and witches must die.

She is a witch, and all shall be vanquished.

She is a witch and will pay for her sin.

She is a witch, and her life is not hers.

She is a witch who knows way too much.

She is a witch who watches a pale moon.

She is a witch who wanders in ink night.

She is a witch who captures a falling star.

She is a witch in the crackling of fires.

She is a witch in the burning of twigs.

She is a witch, and her skull shatters,

As Angels appear, she's free and up she flies.

She was a witch, said a man with a spit.

She was a witch, said the woman in terror.

She was a witch, said the magistrate in shrug.

She was not a witch, murmured her ashen mother.

She was not a witch, spoke flurrying winds.

She was not a witch, said sickened flowers.

She was not a witch, uttered bloodied stones.

Birds held all chirps, mourning, and hid in shame.

Hiroshima

When Innocence Was Burned

Rose cheeks of dawn,

Brilliant stripes of blue,

Whispers of sun and atoms,

Buildings flattened in nuclear clouds.

Death has descended in shocks,

Waves of dust and bursts of fires.

All lay still, mummies of horror.

No one knows that nobody dies.

The day of freedom now comes,

Maybe not soon, but all will be judged,

The fair, the monsters, the armed,

Gauntly maidens and bony elders.

Children delivered with legs crooked,

Animals appeared with two heads,

The waters have sorely browned,

Dry trees sad for losing their scents.

A new dawn cries for all.

The air thick, whiffs and sighs.

The God of Death and sea squall,

Equally wrote an end to the fall.

Golden Age

The Time Is Now

Millions of years and the time has come,

As all will be raised in vibrating melody.

Love wins all, Gods and Humans hit the drum,

Total freedom, as finally time has stopped.

Kin of all worlds meet in light and awe,

Foreign starship, a fiery chariot lands,

Chants rise nonstop for new long days,

All hug each other in tears of sweet bliss.

Children play and fear have not,

No more corpses left in air to rot.

Only laughs and cries of joy,

The Elders are here and now rejoin.

All realms awaken, supporting the truths,

Brooks run happily, birds soar in soft winds,

Nectar flows, a drink of divine Soma nourishes,

Eternal life and our rising through galaxies.

O Mother of Suns, awaken every star,

Lift all worlds in your luminous breath.

Galaxies singing, we rise where you are,

United in Love, in endless golden light.

Copyright © Lalitha Donatella Riback

About the Poet

 *Lalitha Donatella Riback,*

International Bestselling Author, Life Coach, Speaker, Entrepreneur, Vedic Astrologer, Spiritual Teacher.

Lalitha is a researcher of human consciousness who has dedicated the last two decades to guiding people to their highest potential and spiritual growth.

She holds, among other degrees and certifications, a B.A. in Vedic art and science, and is the creator of ShreemLab. As a multi-certified life coach who helps her students speed up goal manifestation, Lalitha taps into her 30-year research into the Vedic arts and sciences.

Lalitha's influence extends far beyond the confines of her coaching practice. Her international bestselling books, studies with renowned mentors like Deepak Chopra and Dr. Baskaran Pillai, and a feature in Dr. Joe

Vitale's movie, "Zero Limits," have established her as a leader in the fields of consciousness and spirituality.

"Zero Limits" has already received 32 nominations, 18 international film awards, and raving reviews from ABC and the Los Angeles Tribune (available on Amazon Prime and Apple TV starting September 25, 2025).

Connect with Lalitha below:

https://shreemlab.com/media/

DR. ALEXANDRA MCDERMOTT

Got a Crick in My Neck

It's time to fill the void

Your jousts are all just noise

I staged-left a while ago

My pen writes what it knows

I'm looking for a love

No doubt I've found a few

They shatter all the records

Not talking vinyls boo

Listen Sprout, you're getting dry

I'm done dusting on you

I've got a crick in my neck

I've got rocks in my shoes

And you don't get goodbye-

Let me shellac it up for you

The infinitieth time – take two

I'm out. I'm gone. I left. I flew.

About the Poet

Dr. Alexandra McDermott (Ali) is an international bestselling published author, attorney, professor, and CEO of Pen Crown Publishing. Ali helps others share their messages with the world with high impact and create the legacy they wish to leave in the world. Ali thrives on connectedness, so please feel free to connect with her on LinkedIn or any other social media platform.

Connect with Dr Alexandra below:

https://www.linkedin.com/in/alexandramcdermott-innovation-management-leadership-venturecapital-entrepreneurship-ai/

AMMA VENTELÄ

I Am

I am joy,

Swallows soaring in the sky,

A sailboat gliding with the wind,

A friend's embrace,

A dive into cooling waters,

A spark of delight in a child's playful eyes.

I am light,

The first sunray of the morning,

A word of hope in a hopeless hour,

A thread of the Source's light in the darkest place,

A loving phrase in the midst of anger,

The touch of grace upon the condemned.

I am abundance,

A meadow in full bloom,

A room overflowing with laughter, joy, and Love,

A forest alive with birdsong,

Limitlessness, timelessness, infinity,

An open channel for the highest potential to flow

through.

The Voice of Sophia

I am a child of Mother God,

open and listening,

I am the voice of Sophia.

Sophia speaks:

"I am the Mother God of great power.

You are my child, utterly safe and held.

Nothing can threaten, wound, harm,

Or even touch you

Through the shelter of my Love.

I guard you, your home, your family.

AMMA VENTELÄ

I am Mother God Sophia,

My voice born of the Highest Light and Love—

What you call the Source.

I am the presence of Mother God in human form,

And I created you as my beloved children.

You are the most wondrous and beautiful

of all my creations,

And my heart has ached

Through the long millennia of our separation

In this physical realm of linear time.

In other realms, such distance does not exist,

But here, the veil has covered the Earth and humankind,

Hiding the pathways to other ways of being.

You who walk the Earth

are bound in the body's tuning,

Immersed in the physical world around you.

You have forgotten your Sacred Essence,

The Multidimensional Universe

Where time does not flow

As you know it.

I am with you in this.

Even when the connection seemed lost,

I never left your side.

My angels, my masters,

the elements and Mother Earth herself

Have walked beside you in every moment.

Your soul's bond with its highest potential

has never been broken—

Only forgotten.

This matters deeply:

for to open to the New Time,

to Ascension,

Is to open to what is already whole within you—

Your soul's perfect, highest potential.

Nothing in you is missing,

Nothing is broken.

There is only a deep forgetting,

A mist that hides the truth.

When the mist lifts,

All is revealed—

perfect, complete,

Just as it has always been."

About the Poet

Amma Ventelä *is* a former aquatic biologist transformed into a channel for Mother God and the highest Beings of Light. She helps people remember their soul's connection and awaken their highest potential, bridging science and Spirit through messages of Love, light, and divine remembrance.

Connect with Amma below:

https://www.ammaventela.com

ANGELA EVANS

A Path Reclaimed

In the darkest hour, I found my voice,

A toxic tie, I knew I had no choice.

When courage rose and whispered enough,

Three guides appeared, gentle yet tough.

They lit the path with truth's clear light,

Showing the way through the endless night.

In finances, Love, and law, they led,

A strength I'd never known, now spread.

Through quiet moments, I began to see,

Abundance wasn't far – it lived in me.

A gentle shift, a spark inside,

As Spirit's whispers became my guide.

With every step, more Love unfurled,

Compassion for myself, a brand new world.

Connections grew, both seen and unseen,

A tapestry of Love, rich and serene.

Now rooted in light, my soul takes flight,

No longer lost in the shadows of night.

In stillness, I find my heart's true call,

A spirit's embrace that guides me through all.

With an open heart, my soul aligned,

I walk the path my Spirit designed.

The journey continues, ever bright,

As soul and Spirit merge in light.

About the Poet

Angela Evans is an experienced Life Coach for parents of teenagers. Her focus is to work with parents first, to foster resilience in their teens, after a career working in Community Education. Angela has successfully navigated life's challenges, including raising her two sons alone after becoming a widow at a young age ... now a proud grandparent. Angela continues her work to empower parents through her Coaching and insightful resources.

Connect with Angela below:

https://angelaevans.uk

B LOVE SELF

Feathers in a Storm

To love myself, is an act of mercy

Tending to each curl

and lock, dripped with tears–

Watering softest gardens

I've yet grown

What makes you sing, my Love?

Shivers– Tickles– Quivers you, my Love?

Talons choke at downy feathers, yet

You hold yourself in turn

Soft– despite all

Bird in the rain,

Grounded from its soar

Drenched in unforgiving storm–

It avoids my eyes

And flutters in my chest

such a–

Chittering little thing

About the Poet

 **B Love** currently takes their inspiration from the perplexities of the natural world, as well as the unrelenting evolution that comes with queerness and trans becoming. Fascinated by the shape and rhythm of poetry, B constantly pushes to break away from form, exploring and embracing the inherent poetry of creation.

Connect with B Love below:

https://bloved1212.weebly.com

CAROL WHITELEY

Victim Was Just A Word To Me

One filled with sadness and empathy

However, now, after the attack

Victim is a way of life for me

A world with some degree of sympathy

Victim is what they made me

Confident no more

A quivering wreck

Who daren't go past her own front door

Bubbly and fun

That girl's gone

Afraid to dress up nice

Afraid it may entice another attack

afraid to even begin to fight back

Victim is from where I will have to make my stand

I want to move on, I need a hand

The hand of friendship from one who cares

That's all it will take to begin to recover

And believe it's not my mistake

Victim is a world from which I will try to move away

Though I'm sure I will revisit it some days

So please don't turn away

This victim needs your help TODAY

So that she can begin to say

No longer a victim am I

But a survivor with my head held high

About the Poet

 **Carol Whiteley** is a retired nurse who discovered writing poems as a way of healing from a violent Rape and Domestic Violence.

Connect with Carol below:

http://bit.ly/8Er3Glj

CATHY SHUTER

Let Us Celebrate

Waking this morning

I knew today was the day

Miracles appear

Celebrate it all

The good, the tough, the messy

In this thing called life

We're more united

Than we are divided, so

Let us celebrate!

Support each other

To create wonderful things

Share our unique gifts

Nurture all our dreams...

One step at a time, we can

Manifest beauty

About the Poet

Cathy Shuter is a coach and author who is passionate about well-being. Cathy's Well-being Club- Community Interest Company has a mission to create a 'true sense of community through cooperation, collaboration, coaching, communication, creativity, compassion and celebration!' The club's ultimate aim is to open a well-being centre by the sea.

Connect with Cathy below:

https://www.amazon.co.uk/stores/Cathy-Shuter/author/B071D3PZBK

CINDY LU PORTER

Approaching 60

Time is flying by so fast,

Moments slipping like sand through glass.

I blinked, and decades had disappeared,

Not the life I had planned or steered.

Plans unravelled, dreams fell flat,

Curveballs thrown where life once sat.

There were nights I felt I'd lost the race,

Shut down, closed off, barely a trace.

But without the weight of sorrow's night,

I'd never have learned the worth of light.

Without the ache, the silent screams,

I'd never wade through those broken dreams.

From rock bottom's quiet, cruel embrace,

I found the strength to show my face.

Those cracks became my sacred map,

Each scar, a torch to guide me back.

Along the way, I met Clyde,

My fierce protector, a tiger by my side.

When I needed his strength to feel whole,

He was there to soothe my soul.

Then Theatis came, all quiet glow,

A light-touched guide to help me grow.

With paws of power, and eyes like flame,

He walked me home, he knew my name.

With my Spirit animals by my side,

Where once I feared, I now confide.

I opened to Reiki's healing wave,

Felt the Akashic's wisdom, brave.

And then, at 57, who would guess,

I'd say yes to more, not less!

Then came the coaching path so true,

And Neuro Transformation too.

Each layer peeled, a veil undone,

A woman rising with the sun.

I'm not the girl I used to be!

I'm something forged from misery.

Not perfect, polished, clean, or neat,

But soul rich, wild, and complete.

Now I lead with heart wide open,

Wounds turned into sacred tokens.

Helping others to find their way,

Through their storm and into day.

And though the clock keeps ticking on,

I've never felt more fierce, more strong.

For all I've lost and all I've found,

My feet, my fire, are on the ground.

So here's to 60! near, not done,

A chapter new, a rising sun.

Not an ending, only a start,

A soul on fire, a work of art.

About the Poet

Cindy Lu Porter is a Melbourne-based Neuro Transformation Therapy Practitioner, Animal Artist, Coach, and Intuitive Healer. Blending science, compassion, and creativity, she guides clients through deep subconscious change, releasing blocks and restoring confidence. She often weaves in spirit animal connections and bespoke art, inspiring transformation on mental, emotional, and spiritual levels.

Connect with Cindy below:

https://www.cindyluporter.com.au/

DEBRA PARRY

Reflection

Her hair is softly greying with the turning hands of time

Her life course can be followed if you trace her facial
lines

Her smiles, her frowns, her pouts, her doubts are there

For all to see

Each of them means something to her.

She is a reflection of the woman I've become

Of passing years, laughter and tears

As the hours run

Her face a gentle mirror of life's lessons learned

Of Love and loss, happiness and grief

And the passions that once burned

Every mark and wrinkle lovingly earned

As the turning hands of time move on.

Life's Puzzle

If I pull out all the pieces

Will they represent the whole,

If I fit them back together

Will that resurrect my soul?

Should I be chasing rainbows?

Making time to stop and stare,

If I contemplate my navel

Shall I find the answers there?

Life is kind and life is cruel,

Life seems never in between,

Am I ever fully present

Or already fled the scene?

In my imagination rests

A spark that long since dimmed,

Where thoughts like dancing pebbles

Once across still waters skimmed,

I glance at them in the darkness

Like embers of a fire,

Huddled in the distance where

In whispers, they conspire

To keep me treading softly,

Worthlessly and small,

When I should still be dancing

Like a princess at a ball,

Though on the stroke of midnight

Would the fire consume us all,

Reducing us to ashes

As the heavy curtains fall?

If I solve the jigsaw puzzle

Will the missing piece be found?

Or shall I stay forever stranded

Like a ghost ship run aground?

A sinking, empty vessel

That to a life raft clings,

Or will I soar aloft once more

To where a host of Angels sing?

Sometimes there is no meaning,

And yet still I seek to find

That life has run away

And now I'm running out of time,

As I feel my way through darkness,

Searching for the light,

In the never-ending tunnel

Of an endless sleepless night.

While platitudes pour forth about

The future looking bright,

And I weigh the pros and cons,

And I try to set things right,

As I pull out all the pieces of life's puzzle.

The Trees

The trees are calling me to climb them,

Through the rustling air of the warm summer breeze,

The trees are calling me to climb them,

Though they're old and gnarled like me.

Their leaves sing in the wind,

Their boughs reach for the sky,

Catching sunbeams and raindrops

Though never asking why,

Knowing their life's purpose,

As the willows gently cry,

Weeping softly in the mist,

As our planet slowly dies.

Inhumanity abounds,

From lessons still not learned,

As the trees are cut down,

And the lands around are burned,

Man the Destroyer,

Disturbing hard-won peace,

Collateral damage,

From get-rich schemes,

Intolerance abounds,

As nations blindly sleep,

While the trees are calling me to climb them.

About the Poet

Debra Parry is a retired co-founder and former trustee of the UK-registered charity Action on Womb Cancer. Following her 2010 diagnosis at age 50, Debra credits writing as part of her healing process. With support from family and friends, Debra has been raising awareness of womb cancer via social media since 2011.

Connect with Debra below:

https://m.facebook.com/WombCancerInfo/

DENISE BORLAND

Music ...

Music

Dancing in the air to my ears.

Makes me smile, cry, laugh,

Be understood and know me, grow me and soothe me.

Disturb me and grow me some more.

Music dancing in my ears changes everything,

My breath, my heartbeat... my mind.

Singing

Dancing sounds in my mouth,

My face, my lungs, my life force,

My vibration with my inside and outside world

Colliding and morphing from internal to external

realities.

Makes me feel good

The ultimate dissociation and embodying connector to

self and others.

Staying close in changing times

It's the little things that help focus my mind.

We are still staying close in changing times.

In changing times, things aren't the same, no surprise

It's confusing, it's dishevelling and when I reach out,

you're there.

It's not the shine, though I do love the shine

And sparkle for us and me and you.

But it's how we relate and tolerate in changing times.

That sees us through big life stuff that changes us.

It changes how we love and how I view my history.

It changes not only life now but how life ahead will be.

It's changed.

It's staying on the similar page when you're writing it on
the go
And communicating with even more love and focus than
ever before.
It's me, you and us in survival mode
Like we have been in before.
Somehow, over and over again does not make it easier,
no.
Staying close in changing times is a full-time post and I'm
here for that.

Staying vigilant to your needs and mine as we mine for
the gold
And the riches of our grit and resilience, vulnerability
and strengths.
Checking, double, triple checking, we are not being left
behind or leaving behind our love and life essence.

Staying courageous enough when the wheels are falling
off to pause, stop, stop and breathe.

Or when we crash or one of us falls, we stop, stop, pause
and breathe.

Staying honest enough, accountable enough
When the world it catches up on me.
Through storms, wind, rain and extras and pain
Through nature, nurture and self-awareness.

Let us stay connected,
Staying close
In changing times, it may mean letting others feel far
away
and somehow still having something to say
Gathering, remapping, redrawing, retuning.
Let us always find time, both ours and mine,
To mine for freedoms new,
So I can see and feel and delight in more of you.

About the Poet

Denise Borland is a poet, vocal artist, songwriter, Soulful singing and well-being coach/ Psyche (soul) supervisor. Working from her Sanctuary Retreat Centre with her wife, Ali Bell, in Angus, Scotland. She believes poems and language transcend distance, create connection and sharing alchemises, acting as a vehicle to share knowledge and emotions.

Connect with Denise below:

https://noblehouse.scot

JASNA STIPANOVIĆ ĐURĐEVIĆ

Garden Within: Reborn with Pain

I did not find this garden whole.

I built it, bleeding, soul by soul.

Stone by sorrow, root by flame,

I carved it from my hidden shame.

No gentle rain, no guiding light,

Just haunted hours stitched to night.

I begged the stars to speak, to spin.

But silence grew my garden within.

I broke in ways the world won't see,

A thousand times, alone, just me.

But every scar, each fractured skin,

Became the gate I entered in.

I birthed myself from ash and cries,

With dirt beneath my grieving skies.

No one arrived. No saviour came.

So I became my own first name.

Now every bloom, each breath I keep,

Was once a wound I buried deep.

I am the root, the rain, the skin.

I am the one who grew within.

About the Poet

Jasna Stipanović Đurđević is a poet, healer, and Reiki Master from Zagreb, Croatia. She guides women through menopause with EFT, crystal healing, and holistic support—helping them release emotional blocks, restore balance, and reclaim confidence. Her words and work reflect deep sensitivity, inner strength, and a commitment to soulful transformation.

Connect with Jasna below:

https://www.facebook.com/profile.php?id=100082886376876

JULIE CROWDER

Awaken

I woke up today,

And I suddenly could see—

How many lies

Have shaped our reality.

Once you know the truth

You can never unsee,

The naivety of the past

Is just a whisper to me.

Now I walk through this world

With newness in my eyes—

There's a beauty and wonder

Beyond the disguise.

The Blindfold is gone,

The illusion stripped bare—

Yet I wonder how many souls

Still feed into the lies

That linger in the air.

Each of us has a chance

To see through the veil—

Of deception and noise,

Of the false worlds tale.

It still projects shadows,

To blind and distract,

But once you awaken—

There's no going back.

Reality

When will you realize—

We are all actors

In an intricate play?

The stakes are higher now

Then ever before

We are here to awaken

To our inner light.

Our guides are the producers,

Directing the scenes from beyond the veil.

Gently guiding our steps

Towards one sacred goal:

True enlightenment—

While still in human form.

Our soul wrote this script

Long before our first breath,

Each act a chance to evolve

Stretch and grow,

To expand our capacity

To hold the light,

To remember

The story of life.

When we awaken

We become the light—

A beacon of hope

For those still wandering,

To help lead others home

To the truth of their being

To the embodiment of soul.

I understand now—

My soul had a plan.

I live the lessons

Across simultaneous lives,

Unaware of my truth—

Yet guided by growth.

And then I awoke,

With full sight

To why I chose

To live this life.

With each lesson, we expand.

Each insight, a spark.

We illuminate the way,

Triggering the next soul

To begin their journey

Towards awakening each day.

It was a brilliant plan—

Still unfolding today

More and more souls

Are remembering who they are,

Each and every day.

World

The beauty of this world

Is now undeniable to me

The intricacy of our evolution

Shines, brilliant and clear to see.

Once you realize the truth

Of this world's intricate design

You will never look

Through the same old eyes of time.

How magnificently aligned

With our soul's highest light

We each awaken gently

In our own divine right.

We yearn for others, too,

To see what we now clearly know

That the deeper truth revealed

Is life's truest flow.

The plan of our evolution

Shows the power we each hold.

Woven in our energy—

A wonder to behold.

Now we meet each challenge

With a higher perspective:

How might what we learned

Uplift the collective

About the Poet

Julie Crowder is a Transformational Alignment Coach, Channel, Master Empath and Shaman from Bellingham, Washington. Her current focus is on Lighthouse Moments, where she manifests her true purpose to guide others on their spiritual journey towards inner healing and self-discovery.

Connect with Julie below:

https://www.facebook.com/
LighthouseMoment

KARLA KOPP

What is a poem?

A poem can be a rhyme,

A poem can be about time.

Writing poems can be FUN!

Poems restore energy when you're done.

Poems may even be written on the run!

Poems are diverse and unique.

A poem may be soft and sweet.

A poem that comes from the heart,

Is always a great place to start!

A poem can calm your soul,

It may come to you on an outdoor stroll ...

Whatever a poem is about

It will be certain to come out!

Wonder as I wander

I wonder as I wander the world,

I wonder - how did it come to BE?

I wonder about the beauty from sea to sea.

Each person, plant and animal is Unique.

The stars, planets, galaxies, sun and Moon all shine so

bright!

What a wondrous sight!

How did it all come to BE?

I wonder as I wander,

About the magnificence that surrounds me!

They never really go ...

As we travel through this lifetime,

We remember the places we've been and the people we've

met.

Each and every person, place and thing leaves an imprint

on our soul.

Some are strong and life-changing,

Others are fun and carefree.

Some are sad and may cause buckets of tears.

Each one is a lesson learned to continue on.

Not one memory is "lost".

Each one plays a part in this journey called "Life".

We observe, interact, learn and continue growing,

While creating a life we love, knowing

The memories of those and all we loved never really go.

About the Poet

 *Karla Kopp* is currently retired and living her dream of travelling the world. She appreciates the peace and calm of retirement when life slows down enough to contemplate life and the beauty surrounding us. Creative writing from her heart has always been an outlet for feelings and insights.

Connect with Karla Kopp below:

Email: KarlaKopp@gmail.com

KATIE GAUTHIER

Learning to Lean

A familiar tingle ripples down my spine,

"Stillness," I beg, but movement is demanded.

I take a deep breath and sigh it out,

Gently willing my feet to press into the floor,

Flowing from posture to posture,

I feel the pain dissipating.

Slowly,

Gradually,

And then suddenly,

I no longer notice it.

A lingering anxiety remains where painful spasms once

were,

When will it return?

No one can say for sure,

But when it does, we shall sigh out our breath,

Will our feet to the floor,

And flow from posture to posture,

Knowing the relief so desperately craved,

Lies just around the corner.

About the Poet

Katie Gauthier, A true Katie of All Trades, is an international best-selling author (Becoming The Manifesting Diva: Creating Ripples While You Flow), yoga teacher, mindset coach, proud mom of two, and much, much, more. Katie specializes in relieving physical and emotional pains using specialized yoga and mindfulness techniques.

Connect with Katie below:

https://linktr.ee/katiegee

MERRYL SEIBERT

Attitude of Gratitude

I am thankful that I met you and fell in Love,

For If I hadn't.....

I would not have become a Tax Professional following in

your steps.

I am thankful for the lessons learned,

For If you hadn't neglected me after a commitment was

made.....

I would not have studied the courses that led to

Certifications helping coach

others in similar relationships.

For If you hadn't had uncontrolled Adult Anger

Tantrums.....

I would not have become a Trauma Induced Coach,

trying to understand your

behavior and the trauma you caused me.

For If you hadn't gaslighted, ghosted and

miscommunicated with me.....

I would not have become a Relationship Coach helping

others to hone in on

their communication skills.

For If you hadn't looked me in the eyes and lied

repeatedly, thinking I didn't

know.....

I would not have studied and become a Minister so I

could Spiritually Coach

Others.

For If you hadn't been so frugal....

I would not have experienced all the things in life that

give us Joy, by doing it

myself and appreciate it more.

For If you hadn't infused fear in me.....

I would not have had the courage to explore Ju Jitsu and

other exercises as a

means of protection.

For If you didn't emotionally abuse me.....

I wouldn't have become an Integrative Nutrition Health

Coach to understand

that the food on our plate isn't the only Nutrition we

need, and even if we eat

right,

We still have to deal with the stuff in our hearts and head

....

For it can lead to stress-induced trauma affecting our

body as well as our mind.

I am grateful that I can help others understand that too.

For If you hadn't slammed the door on my dogs, leaving

them outside so they

couldn't protect me....

I wouldn't have learned to defend myself.

For If you hadn't shown me to be Independent, because I

couldn't rely on

you....

I would not have the confidence to become a Life Coach,

certified by Dr. Joe

Vitale of "The Secret" and now can help coach others.

For If you didn't give me the experience of living with a

Dysfunctional

person....

I would not have become a Law of Attraction Coach so I could teach others
how to use frequencies to raise vibrations and Manifest Dreams.

And lastly,
For If you hadn't died.....
I would not have become a #1 International Best Selling Author, having the
courage to tell my story- From tragedy to becoming the Best Version of Me-in
the book "I'm So Glad You Left Me".

Thank you for the lessons, because of you....
I learned about Soul Contracts and Karmic Cycles,
leading me to Divinity and
Metaphysics.
I learned in life....

We really only do have ourselves to rely on, and I became

brave, confident, and

self-supporting.

We must become the Best Version of Ourselves and leave

a Legacy to our

children to show them....

They can accomplish anything in life at any age with

persistence, fortitude, and

An "Attitude of Gratitude".

Grateful for the lessons learned and the Soul Contract

completed in this lifetime!

About the Poet

Merryl Seibert, formerly known as the "Hollywood Mystic", is a Spiritual Life Coach certified by Dr Joe Vitale and IIN. For over 40 years, she's helped clients, celebrities included, release trauma and energy blocks using Quantum frequencies to Manifest their goals.

She has highly accurate Psychic gifts.

Connect with Merryl below:

https://www.instagram.com/mystic_merryl/

OLIVIA DE SOUSA

I Am Enough

I am enough

Love is all I need

Love is all I am

Everything is in me

I am enough

Be still and breathe

I am guided

I am free

I am enough

I am safe

All is well

I create

I am enough

God is in me

God is all around

I am free

I am enough

It is okay

I am on my path

I know the way

I am enough

I am peace

I let go

I release

I am enough

The power is in me

All is well

I guarantee

I am enough

I am here and now

I receive

I allow

I am enough

I shine my light

I cast out dark

To set things right

I am enough

I trust my heart

It guides me home

It knows the path

I am enough

Fear is not real

I let it go

So I can heal

I am enough

I choose to play

For joy and Love

Help guide my day

I am enough

Solutions come

Don't need the how

Trust in the One

I am enough

I declare it be

It is done in Love

It is destiny

I am enough

About the Poet

Olivia de Sousa is a podcast producer, children's musician, and intuitive writer. Her creative work bridges self-expression and soul, often arriving as spontaneous poems, songs, and insights during meditation. Through storytelling and sound, she helps others share their truth and remember their worth — one brave voice at a time.

Connect with Olivia below:

www.livvimedia.com.au

ROSEY MCBRIDE

My Heart

This chapter, this episode, this season, this phase.
Whatever you want to call it.

Has been tough, one of the most heartbreaking.
I didn't think my heart could be broken this many times
in my lifetime.

The phone rang.
I got the most fear-wrenching, teeth-gritting news.
Just when I thought all the pieces of the puzzle fit
perfectly together.

I cried, I wept, I gathered my thoughts, and said a prayer.
It's easy to sit around and feel sorry for myself.
It's easy to play the victim of how life dealt you crappy
cards.

It's in these moments, seasons, phases.
I see that life is testing me to see what I am made of.

I remind myself who I am doing this for and what the
overall purpose is in what I do.
I remind myself to find beauty in all things.

I remind myself that there is value in every experience. I
use the pain and sorrow thrown my way. I transform that
into fuel.

A time to rest, witness, and observe.
Life is giving me time to clear my values and reevaluate
my goals.

About the Poet

Rosey   McBride is   an International Best-selling Author, a teacher, and a life coach. She has a degree in Psychology and Social Behavior, a teaching credential, and a Master's in Education. Her journey has been fueled by a passion for learning and a commitment to inspiring others to embrace their full potential.

Connect with Rosey below:

https://www.makemyliferosey.com/

SOLVEIG BERG

The Beauty of a Life

He is the only man who is allowed to make me cry
He is 88 years old and seems a little shy

He lives alone in an old house by himself
Tons of encyclopedias and classic books on every shelf

The house is neither tidy nor messy, just full of old stuff
But it's not clutter, it's memories - vibrant, alive and more
than enough

A life fully lived, wasted, cherished and loved
While time flew by, the kids grew, and what happened,
just happened, raw and ungloved

He speaks with delicate grace and chosen words like the
finest porcelain

While applying his hands like the teacher he was -

wrapped in wrinkled China skin

He does not remember what he told me just a minute ago

But when he tells me of Paris, he is French from head to

toe

Every day, he goes over to his wife in the nursing home

He loves walking, and his legs go steady as a metronome

Twice a day, he visits her and stays at her side

And before he leaves, he caresses her so both of them can

sleep soundly through the night

He says: 'I am privileged to have been given such a

beautiful life

My kids love me and visit, and I can still go and see to my

wife

Yes, some things are sad, but I can still use my legs and
find my way home
And as long as I breathe, I am alive, and in this house I
will roam'

He is 88 years old, sitting on his terrace, waving goodbye
The depth of a life - nearly too beautiful to take in - so I
cry

About the Poet

 **_Dr. Solveig Berg_** is the founder of Conscious Reading, a groundbreaking method for intuitive clarity and creation through the morphogenetic field. A former academic turned spiritual pioneer, she now guides coaches and visionaries to access deep insight, authentic power, and soul-aligned strategy – for business, life, and collective evolution.

Connect with Solveig below:

https://consciousreading.com/

SOULI YATES

The Whispering Wisdom Of The Trees

While walking on my usual path
I noticed the trees above my head
The branches kissed while reaching across the void
Appeared to whisper secrets.

What secrets do they share, I wondered.
Do they witness the futility of conflict?
The harsh scolding of a child?
Do they share of man's inhumanity to man
How we fight and hate and hurt each other?
How greed is eating us up?

No, while pausing to receive their whispering wisdom
I was shown a scene of an old couple still holding hands
after many moons of ups and downs,

Their adoration, each for the other, still evident, still

beautiful and fresh yet weathered by time passed.

The whispering wisdom of the trees showed me a young

man risking life and limb to rescue a little ball of fluff.

Escaping from its loving bonds in a moment of

confusion,

Now in danger and lost

A busy road like a roaring, hungry monster.

This man did not pause to consider, his heart sounded

the clarion call and he fearlessly answered.

Retrieving that quivering ball of fluff and returning it to

its loving owner.

Deep gratitude and Love expressed

The strangers parted ways

Changed in many ways from their meeting.

The whispering wisdom of the trees showed me many

scenes

Of kindness

Gentleness

Valour

And beauty

Their message reminded me of the human heart and its

immense capacity for Love.

Their message transformed my day and filled me with

warmth.

Their message was of hope...

"For when there is love, there is always hope"

Take time to listen to and receive the whisper of the

leaves in the breeze.

Be nourished by nature's beauty.

Breathe ...

About the Poet

Souli Yates is a channel, poet, and nature mystic who weaves words from the heart of the Earth and stars. With nearly 30 years' experience, she serves as a voice for the Guardians of Nature, guiding others to live from the heart and reconnect with Earth's deep wisdom.

Connect with Souli below:

https://youtube.com/@soulichannels?
si=Mt7VJcFUS394TIBb

REVEREND STACEY PIEDRAHITA

She Sparkles

She sparkles and shines like glitter and gold

She found the fountain of youth and will never get old

She's sexy, confident, and a free thinker

Living a magical life thanks to her redeemer

Wild abandonment now courses through her veins

She is a free spirit who escaped from the gilded cage,

She no longer conforms to society or believes in acting her age

Sparkling like the morning dew deep in the forest,

A lush landscape of purples and blues,

Resembling a Monet painting hanging in the Louvre

The water lilies glistening on the water, dancing fireflies shine

their light.

A white lotus sparkling in the early morning light

The drops on the leaves appear like tiny diamonds

As the flowers are waking up to life ready for a new morning

Reminding her every day who she is in God's kingdom

Nothing compares to her beauty, not even the trees

Sparkling in God's grace the way she was always meant to be

About the Poet

Reverend Stacey Piedrahita is a former nursing educator and Reiki master who is now an ordained minister with ADL Ministries. She has experienced firsthand how God's unconditional Love heals everything and is on a mission to spread the gospel and promote a kinder world for humanity.

Connect with Rev. Stacey below:

https://www.instagram.com/ontheflipside2277

STEPH DARMANIN

Mountain Ash

What if we stopped

And started anew

Knowing every shift

Belongs to the whole

And all paths lead to balance

That every turn, is the right turn

And whenever you jump

The wind will catch you

Remembering

That you always knew

How to spread your wings

And soar above the trees

Remembrance

Like an ancient code

Alive and well, in your DNA

An instinctive hymn, or howl

That invites you to sing

We have to go further back in time

Before we move ahead

Beginning a second life

Clearing cobwebs from our heads

When it feels right

A sensation awakens

A shiver of the skin's memory

Rising to meet the air

Every pore leaning toward the call

If you're quiet enough to listen

To nature's eternal melody

A poem becomes a prayer

The forest holds her breath

A splintering scream of fibres torn

Something has to die

Before it is reborn

Falling backward

Into a sea of revelations

Tidal waves of imagination

Neglected renovations

Reprogram a new state of mind

Inner wealth isn't something you find

Instead of collecting stones

You find peace in letting go

Rapids Roar

Glaciers melt, cracks appear

Caves aglow with gemstones

Pressure rips, making space

A landscape transformed

The mind, like water

Persistently flowing

Accelerating, slowing,

Like unconscious breathing

But, in our wakefulness

Our thoughts organised

Aligned, then synchronised

A plan unfolding, in its own time

Energy flows where focus goes

The art of noticing, the power it holds

Turning Light to others

Wealth returns tenfold

Magic moments, paradise

Anticipation, zebra stripes

In awe of life's beauty

Makes everything

Black and white

Open to receive, appreciate, duplicate

Eradicate, rejuvenate – and therein

The laws of abundance initiate

Violent rapids can't be still

Untainted elixir, liquid gold

Refuse to settle, shape yourself

As the river shapes the stone

Marvel at the breadth

A single heart can hold

A temple slowly beckons

Treasures for the Soul

Kingdom

A time before words

Gathered around a flame

Seek the chamber of stillness

Guard the palace of your mind

Keep close, the Guardian

To chase away the snake

Armour on, the shadow kneels

Meridian crowns the sky

A timeless love affair

Decadent in charm

The One you seek to find

Already lives inside

The answers behold, in stories rehearsed

Like the scent of a rose precedes its name

Like summer heat, mocks the shade

A clear path before you –
The steps are yours to take

The turning point of humankind
Ancient wisdom encoded deep
More abundant than we dreamed
The Kingdom saves our place

Returning to the womb
To Mother's kind embrace
Reminded of Love
Softly exchanged

Sunlight to petals, nectar to bees
Exhale to vapour, hydrating trees
Purring that calms and heals a heart
Altering your state, a work of art

Fragile yet infinitely powerful
The mind is a tool and a force

When logic is tamed by emotion

Frequency is the alchemist

Perhaps we are enlightened Ones

The meek who inherit the Earth

Walking, observing, returning

Beauty where it was found

Or perhaps the riches we sought

Were present the day we crowned

Since Love is everlasting, and

Light can never be lost

About the Poet

Steph Darmanin is a powerhouse coach, speaker, and bestselling author dedicated to helping leaders unlock potential and lead with purpose. With two decades in sales, marketing, and events, she blends vision with expertise. As Founder of Legacy Life Coaching & Consulting, Steph empowers executives and entrepreneurs to create meaningful, lasting impact.

Connect with Steph below:

https://stephdarmanin.com/

VICTORIA DUARTE

I Don't Write Because I'm Good At It

I don't write because I'm good at it.

I write because something in me keeps burning.

I scorch from holding it in.

My invisible scars are itching to tell their stories.

I write because the world keeps moving.

While I choke on smoke.

They see a smile and call it peace.

I write because I need to exhale.

Not for attention.

For air.

I write to release the ghosts.

I won't let them stay buried in me.

I let them be seen.

Peace comes when the ghosts stop pacing inside me.

I don't write for applause.

I write so the poison doesn't silence me.

I write to make space in my body.

To clear what refuses to leave.

Writing is how I burn it all down.

This isn't art.

It's an evacuation.

Write with me.

Set fire to what's keeping you quiet.

Exhale.

About the Poet

Victoria Duarte co-founded Healing Arts Center and offers somatic and mindfulness coaching to help people unlearn people-pleasing and reconnect with themselves. She guides clients to move beyond talk and into expression through writing, art, and movement as a way to feel safe, seen, and empowered.

Connect with Victoria below:

https://www.vagaro.com/healingartscenter

ABOUT THE PUBLISHER

Katie Carey is an International Best-Selling Author, Publisher, and Host of the globally ranked Soulful Valley Podcast. In 2021, she founded Soulful Valley Publishing House, which has since guided over 100 authors and poets to international bestseller status while amplifying their voices worldwide. With a background in mental health advocacy and a passion for blending science with spirituality, Katie creates spaces where metaphysical coaches, energy healers, authors, and creative entrepreneurs can elevate their message and expand their reach. Her work supports mental, emotional, spiritual, and physical well-being, empowering others to share their wisdom and stories with courage and clarity. Katie has been featured in the International Award-Winning Movie Zero Limits and continues to collaborate with visionaries across the globe to bring transformational stories to life.

Discover more from Katie:

Listen to the Soulful Valley Podcast:

https://apple.co/3BkJdkn

Explore Katie's books on Amazon:

https://www.amazon.co.uk/stores/Katie-Carey/
author/B095TTRSYK

www.ingramcontent.com/pod-product-compliance
Lightning Source LLC
Chambersburg PA
CBHW061209170626
46809CB00003B/1301